# The Cavekids Come to Dinner
## Paleo Diet Adventure for Kids

© 2015

ISBN 13: 978-1494295998
ISBN 10: 1494295997

Blog: cavekidscometodinner.com
E-mail: cavekidscometodinner@gmail.com

For Katy and Marianna

Chloe and Dylan Newton lived with their parents, a dog, and a cat in a small town in a house by the lake.

Chloe and Dylan were picky eaters. Instead of fresh homemade meals served by their mom, they would choose to eat food packaged in cans, bags, and boxes. Their tummies hurt, and they were often cranky.

One weekend the kids were playing in the attic when suddenly Chloe noticed a large, strange-looking wooden box with a bench and seatbelts. "That's an unusual piece of furniture! How come we never saw it before?" Chloe took a deep breath and blew off the dust. "What is this, Dylan?"

"I guess it was hidden behind all those things mom donated last week. I think this is what great-grandpa used to work on."

They examined the object closely, analyzing each button and rod.

"Hey, Chloe, check this out! Look, there are some gears inside. I see a cord. Plug it in!"

"Let's play train! All aboooooard! Get into your seats and buckle up, passengers. Our train is departing!" announced Chloe.

"Let's see what happens if I pull on that lever," said Dylan.

Suddenly, they were spinning around and around.

"Aaaaaaaaaah, Dylaaaan, what's going on? It's so dark..."

A few minutes later...

"Where are we, Dylan? What have we done?"

"Oh, Chloe, I have a bump on my head, and it hurts. I think I'm hallucinating... I see a rainforest."

"Well, I see it too, Dylan."

They looked around. They didn't recognize anything around them. Their house had disappeared, and instead they were looking at some kind of jungle.

The kids could smell something appetizing being cooked that reminded them of barbecue. They followed the aroma.

"Look, Chloe— there's a cave over there. Let's go check it out."

"We better be careful. All this seems very strange. Let's go home."

"But where *is* home, Chloe? I don't think we have much choice. We need to find out what's going on here."

They tiptoed toward the cave and peeked inside.

To their huge surprise, they saw a family: a mother, a father, and two young children—a girl and a boy about the same age as them. The children were happily playing, and their parents looked friendly.

The family members were dressed in unusual outfits—furs of some kind. The family was gathered around a fire. A large chunk of meat was sizzling over the flame.

"Dylan, it smells so yummy..."

"Chloe, this looks like some kind of a camping trip, but I'm not sure why they're dressed like that. It's too early for Halloween. Maybe it's a costume party or something..."

"Well, they look like a nice family. I think they would tell us how to get back home. They must have a GPS or a map. Let's go ask them."

The two children approached the family, and Dylan spoke up first. "Hello, I'm Dylan, and this is Chloe. We're lost. Would you please tell us how to get to the closest town?"

"Also, could we please use your cell phone? We need to call our parents," added Chloe politely.

The family seemed puzzled. The adults looked at each other as if they could not understand what these young strangers were asking them.

Confused, Chloe and Dylan were about to leave, when the woman addressed them warmly. "Why don't you join us for dinner?"

Dylan turned to his sister. "Chloe, I'm hungry. I'm not sure what happened to us. I can't explain all this. Maybe we can try some of their food. It does smell good!"

The boy dressed in furs who looked like the older one of the two children approached to more closely examine the new kids.

He squinted and said, "I'm Heidrek, and this is my sister, Vikka, our mom, Tofa, and our dad, Leif."

Chloe and Dylan sat down next to the fire. Tofa handed each of them a flat, wide stone with a few juicy chunks of meat on it.

"This is some kind of exotic meat, something we've never tried before," whispered Dylan to Chloe, chewing a piece of meat. "Maybe it's deer meat or wild boar...I've heard on the news they even sell crocodile meat in supermarkets nowadays..."

"Mm-hmm," was all Chloe could say, her mouth full.

After a good meal, Chloe and Dylan cheered up. The exhaustion from the trip was gone too! They joined the game the new kids were playing. Heidrek and Vikka were very energetic. Chloe and Dylan had a lot of fun with them playing tag and hide-and-seek.

When it started getting dark, Chloe expressed her concern: "Hey, Dylan, I asked Vikka what meat we were eating, and she said that her father just hunted a mammoth. What does it all mean?"

"I've been thinking, Chloe. I remember dad talking about it. The thing we found in the attic was a time-travel machine that our great-grandpa created. The machine obviously worked and took us back a million years in time."

"A million years?...No wonder we were so hungry!"

"Yes, Chloe. These people are cavemen, and the children are cavekids."

"Caveman? Is that, like, their last name? Like our neighbor—Mr. Coleman?"

"Well...something like that..."

"But how are we getting back home, Dylan?"

"Since we have the time-travel machine, we can go back home any time, Chloe."

"But how would we get it to start? There is nowhere to even plug it in. I don't think they've got electricity."

"When we arrived here, I took a good look at our 'vehicle.' There are solar panels on the machine. This means it can run on the sun's energy. Great-grandpa thought of everything."

"So let's go home then!"

"Chloe, we can leave any time, but this is a unique opportunity, don't you see? Seriously, how often do you get to meet cave people?"

"But Dylan, our parents will worry," reminded Chloe in an alarmed voice.

"No problem," answered Dylan. "I thought of that too. I don't want to scare mom and dad, either. When we were playing hide-and-seek, I hid inside the machine. I found instructions in a small compartment that tell you how the machine works. There is a safer landing option, by the way. So I figured, on our return trip, we'll just set the arrival time for the same time we left, and nobody will even notice that we were away."

"Dylan, you are just as much of a genius as our great-grandpa was!" exclaimed Chloe. "We're saved!"

Soon Tofa prepared beds of dry grass for Dylan and Chloe, and the children fell asleep.

The next day they woke up early and went to the woods with their new friends to collect some food. Vikka and Heidrek showed Chloe and Dylan how to look for edible berries, fruits, roots, mushrooms, and nuts.

When they came back, their mouths started watering—Tofa roasted a large bird over a fire. Dylan and Chloe tasted it. It was delicious.

"Mr. Caveman, did you really hunt down a mammoth?" asked Chloe, finishing her meal.

Leif, surprised by how Chloe addressed him, answered her question. "Yes, but I did not do it alone. It was a collective effort."

Day after day Chloe and Dylan were living in the cave; gathering dry wood and foods; helping with keeping the fire, cooking, and cleaning; or just playing with Heidrek and Vikka.

Using sticks, stones, and small animal bones, the cavekids taught Dylan and Chloe many interesting games they had never heard of before.

Heidrek carved two wooden pendants for his new friends: one of Chloe and Vikka, the other of himself and Dylan.

Chloe and Dylan learned how to climb trees and find birds' eggs for their meals. Sometimes Leif took all four children fishing. They used hooks made of bone for catching small fish and a spear for large fish.

Dylan and Chloe noticed that they became much stronger and healthier. Their cheeks turned pink, and they had no more tummy aches.

Their spirits were up, and they were happy.

Time flew by quickly. There was no calendar. To count the days, Dylan put a stone next to the entrance of the cave each morning at sunrise. One morning there were thirty stones sitting there.

Dylan and Chloe didn't want to leave, but they were missing their parents and friends. It was time to go back home.

"Dylan, I'm going to miss Vikka and Heidrek."

"I know, Chloe. I will too, but there's nothing we can do. Unless...nah, it's a pretty far-out idea." He paused. "But maybe they can go with us?"

"I think it's a *great* idea! Now we know how they live. I'm sure they'd be interested in doing the same—seeing how we live. I think the machine can fit the four of us. There are only two seats in the machine, but they are adult size, so four kids would easily fit in there. And we can take them back to their home after they visit us!"

"Well, if their parents let them," said Dylan.

"We think Heidrek and Vikka could learn so much by visiting you," agreed Leif.

"Vikka and Heidrek know how to take good care of themselves," added Tofa.

"Yes! We are going to the future with Chloe and Dylan!" rejoiced Vikka. Heidrek was thrilled too.

Chloe and Dylan collected souvenirs to take with them—herbs, flowers, as well as dry mushrooms and some mammoth jerky.

"OK, everybody," shouted Dylan. "It's travel time!"

All four children hugged Leif and Tofa.

"Goodbye, Mrs. and Mr. Caveman!" yelled Chloe, boarding the time-travel machine.

The kids buckled up and were gone in a second.

"We're home!" Chloe was filled with endless joy. "Mom! Dad! We missed you so much!"

"You didn't see us for half an hour and you already miss us? This is something new!" said Mrs. Newton.

The parents noticed two new children dressed in furs.

"And who are these young lady and gentleman?" asked Mr. Newton in surprise.

Talking in a hurry and interrupting each other, Dylan and Chloe tried to explain what had happened. Their parents had a hard time believing the story, but after talking to the cavekids and examining the unknown herbs, flowers, and strange-looking meat, they realized Chloe and Dylan were not making it up.

"Well, welcome, kids," said Mrs. Newton. "Vikka can stay in Chloe's room, and Heidrek can stay in Dylan's. Chloe and Dylan, you have plenty of clothes. Please, offer some things from your wardrobes to your friends."

"Let's take a tour! This is my room, and this is Dylan's room." Chloe was chirping, busily running around the house. "And these are our pets—Bella and Aiko. See, humans eventually domesticated dogs and cats!"

The next day Chloe and Dylan went back to eating their regular meals—the food from packages. They introduced their food to their new friends. The kids had a picnic at the nearby park.

"It doesn't even look anything like food!" said Vikka suspiciously, biting a small piece of a potato chip. "It tastes pretty good though," she concluded.

"And I like this sweet water with bubbles!" Heidrek was drinking soda.

That afternoon all four kids got tummy aches and felt tired, weak and sleepy.

"What's going on, Dylan?" asked Chloe.

"I think it's the food. We did not have one tummy ache when we visited Heidrek and Vikka and ate their food. We need to do some research."

Chloe and Dylan got to their computers and started searching the Internet for answers. After a couple of hours of exploring, they shared their findings with each other.

"This is what I've learned, Dylan: Most modern foods are highly processed. They are also called 'convenience foods.' They come in boxes, bags, and cans. When you look at the ingredients listed on many packaged foods, there are all kinds of chemicals there that aren't good for us. The companies that process these foods add chemicals to them so that the food can stay on the shelves longer and taste and look better, but the processing makes the food unhealthy. Dylan, the food is making us sick!"

"This is what I've learned, Chloe: The time machine took us to the historical period called the Paleolithic era. We were eating a Paleolithic diet while visiting there, or Paleo diet for short. People used to eat like that for millions of years. This food kept people healthy for many generations."

After doing more research, Chloe and Dylan found Dr. Sage. She was a children's doctor, specializing in nutrition. The kids asked their parents to make an appointment with Dr. Sage.

"Dr. Sage, we often have tummy aches," complained Chloe.

"Kids, if you have any health problem, the first thing to do is to look at your diet. What you eat is very important. Food is the fuel your body runs on. It needs to be high quality in order for you to stay healthy, strong, and active."

"Dr. Sage, we think our tummies hurt because we are eating foods that aren't good for us," shared Dylan.

"I think you are right, kids. You see, there is a whole hidden world inside our bodies. Billions of tiny microorganisms live inside us. Their world is called a *microbiome*. Some microorganisms in our bodies are very helpful for us—they keep us healthy. Other kinds of microorganisms can weaken our bodies and make us feel sick. There is a whole army of good microorganisms—let's call them 'good guys.' They protect us from all the 'bad guys.' Their favorite place to live is in our digestive system. When you eat, the food gets down to your digestive tract and feeds these microorganisms inside you."

Dylan and Chloe were listening intently.

"They eat whatever you eat," continued Dr. Sage. "'Bad guys' *love* eating processed foods and sugars. It makes them strong. If they grow and multiply, they can outnumber the 'good guys.' When this happens, we feel sick, weak, cranky, and tired. But if you eat a healthy diet, the good guys get stronger and keep the bad guys under control."

"Who are these good guys?" asked Dylan.

"There are many kinds of beneficial microorganisms, but some of the most helpful residents in our digestive tract are good bacteria," replied Dr. Sage. "They do many important things for us, such as improve our digestion, manufacture vitamins, and boost our immunity."

"How can we make sure we have good bacteria in our tummies?" inquired Chloe.

"Good bacteria help to ferment foods. If you eat these fermented foods often, you will have enough good microorganisms in your body to keep you healthy."

"Dr. Sage, what are these fermented foods?" Chloe asked.

"For example, sauerkraut is fermented cabbage, which is a traditional dish in Germany; kimchi is fermented Napa cabbage, popular in Korea; gravlax is raw salmon cured in salt, which is one of the menu favorites in Sweden; and beet kvass is fermented beet beverage, enjoyed in Russia. But you don't need to travel all over the world to try these foods. Fermented foods are easy to prepare wherever you are!"

"Besides fermented foods, what foods will keep us healthy?" asked Dylan.

"Foods our ancestors used to eat for millions of years are the most suitable for us. Human bodies evolved on those foods and know best how to use them for fuel. Here is the list of these foods," said Dr. Sage, handing a sheet of paper to Dylan. It read as follows:

- meat, fowl, fish, shellfish, eggs
- vegetables (except potatoes and corn) and mushrooms
- seeds and nuts
- fats: butter, ghee (clarified butter), lard, and tallow from pastured animals, olive oil, coconut oil
- fresh fruits and berries, preferably tart, in moderation

"Of course," continued Dr. Sage, "our modern whole foods are not exactly the same as those that were around a million years ago. Food evolved with people. These are the modern versions of the foods that our ancestors ate. But we have even more healthy food choices now than ancient people had. And here are some healthy and easy recipes for you." Dr. Sage passed a small booklet to the kids. "You can also improvise and create your own recipes."

"Thank you, Dr. Sage." Chloe got up off her seat.

"We've learned so much!" said Dylan.

"Chloe, look at the list of healthy foods! I knew it! These are the same kinds of foods that we used to eat when we visited Heidrek and Vikka," said Dylan as they left Dr. Sage's office. "Remember, Leif hunted and fished, and we went looking for birds' eggs, edible plants, berries, mushrooms, and nuts?"

"It's the Paleo diet!" guessed Chloe.

Excited, Chloe and Dylan rushed home. They couldn't wait to share what they had learned with their friends.

"Heidrek! Vikka! Now we know why we've been feeling so sick lately! And we know how to help!" exclaimed Chloe.

"Here is the plan. Starting today we'll be eating like we were eating at your home," proposed Dylan. "Everybody, let's go 'hunting'! Our first stop is the farm!"

"Look, there are chickens...and pigs...and sheep...and goats! And here is a cow!" Chloe was running around in excitement. "Let's pet the cow!"

Later Vikka and Chloe went to collect eggs from the chicken coop.

"Feel them; the eggs are still warm," whispered Vikka, trying not to alarm the hens.

The kids brought home eggs, bacon, lard, sausages, vegetables, fruits, and big smiles on their faces.

"Vikka! Heidrek! Let's get our aprons on and start cooking!" yelled Dylan.

"Mom! Dad! We've got Paleo recipes!" Chloe was delighted.

The kids worked hard and followed the recipes. Dylan and Chloe's mom and dad helped a bit. Things didn't go smoothly right away, but in the end, the Paleo barbecue dinner turned out delicious.

Day after day, Chloe, Dylan, Heidrek, and Vikka were trying new recipes and changing them and experimenting. It was so much fun! They designed their favorite recipes and gave their own names to them: Heidrek's Poached Salmon, Dylan's Mix-and-Match Meat Skewers, Chloe's Apples with Savory Filling, and Vikka's Tomatoes with Pumpkin and Bacon.

A week passed by...

"Our next stop is the farmers market!" announced Dylan.

The cavekids could not believe their eyes when they saw the abundance of food at the farmers market.

"We've never seen so many kinds of fruits and vegetables," said Heidrek in astonishment.

The kids filled their bags with fresh fruits, vegetables, and mushrooms. They also bought eggs from pasture-raised chickens and some wild-caught fish.

"It seems you brought half of the farmers market home," said Mrs. Newton with a smile when she saw the kids carrying heavy bags.

Vikka, Chloe, Dylan, and Heidrek got busy cooking.

All four kids got well again. Healthy and energetic, they were spending their summer playing in the park, hiking, and swimming in the lake.

Another week passed by...

"Our next stop is the health food store!" said Dylan.

Once again, Heidrek and Vikka were amazed to see a large variety of fresh foods.

"Most fruits, veggies, and mushrooms in this store are organic," said Dylan. "It means they were grown without toxic chemicals, just like the food that we ate while visiting Vikka and Heidrek. These are grass-fed meats and pasture-raised chickens," continued Dylan, pointing at the meat and poultry counter. "This means they are from animals that grazed outdoors, just like animals at Heidrek and Vikka's home. And these birds had a chance to eat insects, like birds do in the wild."

VEGETABLES    FISH    MEAT    POULTRY

ORANGES    PEACHES    BLUEBERRIES

The kids came home with bags full of food. There was much cooking to do.

The summer was coming to an end, and school was about to start. The cavekids missed their parents and became more homesick with each passing day. It was time for them to say good-bye to Chloe and Dylan.

"We'll miss you. Promise you'll visit us again." Vikka was trying to hold back her tears.

"Before we take you home, there is one more thing we need to do," said Dylan in a secretive voice. "You gave us the best present—the Paleo diet—so here is the best present we can give you."

Chloe was carrying a large basket. She pulled the towel off the top. A puppy and a kitten were peeking curiously at the kids.

"They are wonderful! What should we call them?" asked Vikka, gently picking up the kitten.

"I have an idea," said Dylan. "We'll name the puppy Pal, and we'll call the kitty Leo!"

"How creative!" exclaimed Vikka.

"We like it!" laughed Heidrek.

"The Paleo diet is our gift from the past, and Pal and Leo are your gifts from the future!" said Dylan with a smile.

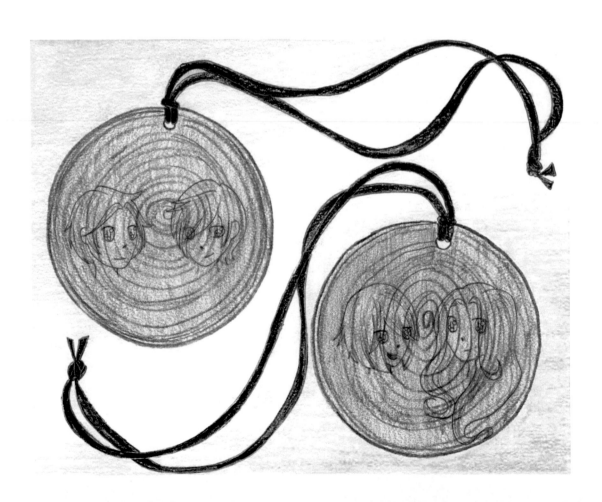

# Paleo Recipes

# "Mushroom Meadow" Eggs

## Ingredients

- 4 hardboiled eggs
- 2 tablespoons ghee (or fat of choice: lard, tallow, coconut oil, etc.)
- ¼ pound finely chopped mushrooms
- ½ cup finely chopped leeks
- 1–2 garlic cloves, finely chopped
- ¼ cup finely chopped dill
- 2 tablespoons homemade mayonnaise
- 4 tomatoes (preferably Campari or ones similar in size)
- Spinach or basil leaves to garnish
- Salt and pepper to taste

**Tip:** You can use tomatoes of different colors to create a pretty "meadow."

## Preparation

1. Sauté leeks in ghee for about 5 minutes.
2. Add mushrooms and sauté for 10 more minutes. Take off the heat to cool.
3. Peel the eggs. Cut the top ⅓ of the eggs off. Carefully remove the yolks.
4. In a bowl, smash the yolks with a fork.
5. Add leeks/mushroom mixture, garlic, dill, mayonnaise, salt, and pepper.
6. Fill egg whites with the mixture.
7. Cut the bottom ⅓ of the tomatoes off. Remove some of the insides of each tomato top.
8. Cover each egg with a tomato "mushroom" cap.
9. Garnish a plate with leaves and carefully set "mushrooms" on top.

# Mayonnaise

## Ingredients

- 3 egg yolks
- 2–3 tablespoons fresh lemon juice
- 1 cup mild olive oil
- 1 teaspoon mustard
- 2 tablespoons raw apple cider vinegar
- 1–2 garlic cloves
- Salt to taste

**Tip 1:** Make sure all ingredients are at room temperature.

**Tip 2:** Use a stick blender and mix the ingredients in the jar in which you are going to keep your mayonnaise. You will have fewer dishes to clean.

**Tip 3:** As a fun touch, you can create mayonnaise of different colors by adding these optional ingredients to it: spinach powder to make green mayonnaise; paprika to make orange mayonnaise; or turmeric powder for yellow mayonnaise.

## Preparation

1. Put all ingredients in a jar.

2. Using a stick blender, mix the ingredients until mayonnaise consistency is reached (1 minute or less).

3. Keep refrigerated.

# Eggs in Cocottes (Mini Pots)

## Ingredients

**For one 8-ounce cocotte (or ramekin):**

- 2 eggs
- 1 strip of bacon, cooked and crumbled
- 1 plum tomato, cut in thin round slices
- 1 tablespoon ghee (or fat of choice).
- 1 tablespoon fresh chopped dill
- Pinch of paprika
- Salt and pepper to taste

 **Tip:** If you prefer the yolks to be soft, bake without a lid. For cooked-through yolks, cover with a lid while baking.

## Preparation

1. Melt ghee in a cocotte.

2. Place tomato slices on the bottom of the cocotte.

3. Add some dill.

4. Sprinkle with salt and pepper.

5. Add bacon.

6. Crack eggs into the cocotte, taking care to keep the yolks intact.

7. Sprinkle with salt and paprika.

8. Bake in preheated oven at 300°F for 15–20 minutes or until the eggs are set to your liking.

# Romaine Lettuce Tacos

## Ingredients

- 1 medium avocado
- 3 tablespoons homemade mayonnaise
- 5 large romaine lettuce leaves
- 5 strips of lox (smoked salmon)
- 10 cherry tomatoes, quartered
- 5 tablespoons fresh chopped dill
- 3 tablespoons chopped scallions
- Salt and pepper to taste

## Preparation

1. Trim thick parts of the lettuce leaves to make them thinner and easier to roll.
2. Mix avocado with mayonnaise in a bowl.
3. Spread the avocado/mayonnaise mixture on the leaves.
4. Arrange the rest of the ingredients at one end of the leaf.
5. Carefully roll each leaf, making sure the ingredients stay inside.
6. Secure each taco with a toothpick.

# Eggs in Avocado Boats

Avocado "boats" are a creative and surprising way to serve eggs. This dish makes for an easy and interesting breakfast. Baked avocado has a smoky flavor.

## Ingredients

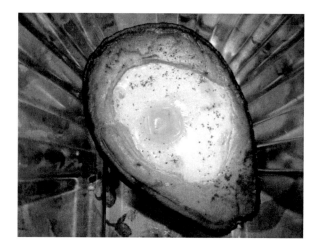

- 1 large avocado
- 2 eggs
- Pinch of paprika
- Salt and pepper to taste

## Preparation

1. Cut avocado in half length-wise.
2. Carefully remove the pit.
3. Remove some of the avocado pulp.
4. Crack eggs into the avocado halves.
5. Sprinkle avocado "boats" with pepper, salt, and paprika.
6. Bake in preheated oven at 300°F for 20–30 minutes or until eggs are set to your liking.

# Vikka's Tomatoes with Pumpkin and Bacon

## Ingredients

- 4 tomatoes
- 4 strips of bacon, cooked and crumbled
- 1 cup of pumpkin (or sweet potato), diced in pieces the size of a raisin
- 1 egg
- 1 onion, finely chopped
- 3 tablespoons ghee (or fat of choice)
- 1 tablespoon chives, chopped
- Salt and pepper to taste

## Preparation

1. Sauté pumpkin and onion in ghee for 5–10 minutes.
2. Transfer to a bowl.
3. Add bacon, salt, and pepper.
4. Beat an egg and add it to the mixture. Mix well.
5. Cut the top ⅓ of the tomatoes off. Hollow out the tomatoes.
6. Fill the tomatoes with the prepared mixture.
7. Carefully transfer stuffed tomatoes into a greased baking dish.
8. Bake in preheated oven at 300°F for 20–30 minutes.
9. Garnish with chives.

# Fruit-Infused Water

## Ingredients

- 1 sliced lemon
- 1 cup diced pineapple or
  1 cup sliced strawberries
- 1 sliced cucumber
- 1 teaspoon finely chopped ginger
- 2 mint leaves
- 2 quarts of filtered water

 **Tip**: prepare it in the evening and refrigerate overnight.

## Preparation

Put all ingredients into a pitcher and refrigerate.

# Chloe's Apples with Savory Filling

## Ingredients

- 4 large apples
- ½ pound of ground meat, preferably a mixture of any of the following: beef, lamb, pork, chicken, or turkey
- 1 small onion, chopped
- 1 sprig of parsley, chopped
- 2 tablespoons ghee (or fat of choice)
- 1 tablespoon raisins
- ⅓ cup chicken broth
- Salt to taste

## Preparation

1. In a skillet, brown ground meat, onion, and parsley in ghee.
2. Add raisins, salt, and broth. Simmer for 5 minutes. Remove from heat.
3. Peel and core apples; hollow them out.
4. Arrange apples in a greased baking dish and fill with the meat mixture.
5. Bake in preheated oven at 300°F for 40–60 minutes.

# Chicken Breast with Fruit Filling

## Ingredients

- 2 chicken breasts
- 2 tablespoons finely chopped walnuts
- 1 peeled apple, minced (or 3 fresh apricots, halved)
- 2 tablespoons ghee (or fat of choice)
- 1 teaspoon ground cinnamon
- ½ teaspoon ground nutmeg
- Pinch of paprika
- Salt and pepper to taste

## Preparation

1. In a bowl, mix apple, walnuts, spices, and salt.
2. Make a slit in a side of each chicken breast, creating a pocket.
3. Stuff it with the prepared mixture.
4. Secure with toothpicks.
5. Spread ghee on top of each chicken breast and sprinkle with paprika.
6. Bake in preheated oven at 300°F for 30–40 minutes.
7. Remove toothpicks before serving.

# Sauerkraut

## Ingredients

- 2 medium-size heads of cabbage
- 2 large carrots
- 2 tablespoons sea salt or Himalayan salt

**Tip 1:** If you don't own a fermenting crock, you can use a glass jar. The trick is to keep the contents submerged in juice with a press.

**Tip 2:** You can make your own press. Find a rock that is slightly smaller in size than your jar's mouth. Boil the rock for 10–15 minutes. Let it cool before use.

## Preparation

1. Reserve one of the outer cabbage leaves for later use.
2. Shred the cabbage. Place it into a large bowl and sprinkle with salt. Press/massage cabbage with your hands until it starts giving juice. You can also use a kraut pounder or potato masher.
3. Grate the carrot and mix with the shredded cabbage.
4. Pack the vegetables into a 2-quart canning jar.
5. Place the reserved cabbage leaf on top of shredded vegetables. Put press on top of the cabbage leaf to keep everything submerged in the cabbage juice. Cabbage will give off more juice over the next few hours. Occasionally, the cabbage can be too dry and won't produce enough juice. If the level of liquid doesn't rise after a few hours, add filtered water to cover the vegetables.
6. Cover the mouth of the jar with a cloth and secure it with a rubber band.
7. Put the jar in a dark place and keep at room temperature.
8. Check on your sauerkraut a couple of times a day to make sure it remains submerged in liquid.
9. Ferment for 3–6 days, starting to taste it on day 3.
10. When sauerkraut taste is to your liking, remove the press, screw the cap on, and refrigerate. It is ready to eat, but because this is a live fermentation, it can keep for a long time. It will continue fermenting under refrigeration, but much slower.

# Golubtsi
# (Russian Stuffed Cabbage)

## Ingredients

- 1 large head of cabbage
- 1 pound ground meat, preferably a mixture of any of the following: beef, lamb, pork, chicken, or turkey
- 1 small head of cauliflower, cut into uniform pieces
- 1 carrot, finely shredded
- 2 tablespoons parsley or cilantro, chopped
- 1 onion, finely chopped
- 2–3 cloves of garlic, minced
- 2 tablespoons ghee (or fat of choice)
- 1 jar (7 ounces) tomato paste
- Salt and pepper to taste

## Preparation

1. Place cabbage in a pot. Pour hot water over it to fully submerge it. Cook over medium heat for about 5 minutes to soften the leaves.

2. Drain the water. Let the cabbage cool.

3. Gently peel off the leaves, trying not to damage them. Trim thick parts of the leaves to make them thinner and easier to fold.

4. Cut stem and leaves off cauliflower. Using a food processor, shred the cauliflower into pieces the size of grains of rice.

5. Sauté onion and carrot in ghee for 5–10 minutes. Transfer to a bowl.

6. Add ground meat, cauliflower, garlic, fresh herbs, salt, and pepper. Mix well.

7. Put 1–2 tablespoons of the meat mixture on a cabbage leaf, closer to one end. Fold two sides and roll along the leaf stem. Using the same method, stuff the desired number of cabbage leaves.

8. Arrange the golubtsi in a pot. Add ghee, tomato paste, and a pinch of salt to the pot.

9. Add hot water to cover the golubtsi.

10. Cover with a lid and cook in preheated oven at 300°F for 1 hour.

# Dylan's Mix-and-Match Meat Skewers

## Ingredients

- 2 pounds of any of the following: beef, lamb, pork, chicken, or turkey (mix and match)
- 2 red bell peppers, cut into 1-inch pieces
- ½ a peeled pineapple, cut in 1-inch chunks
- 3 small onions, cut into rings
- 1 tablespoon chipotle powder (optional)
- 3 kiwis
- 10 grape tomatoes
- Salt and pepper to taste

 **Tip:** If you are barbecuing, start with searing the meat over the fire—hold your meat skewer over a flame for several seconds. The meat will develop a thin crust, and its juices will be locked in.

## Preparation

1. Prepare marinade: In a bowl, mash peeled kiwis with a fork. Add onions, chipotle powder, salt, and pepper.

2. Cut meat in 1-inch chunks and mix with marinade. Refrigerate overnight.

3. Heat your grill to medium-high heat.

4. Thread the skewers, alternating pieces of meat, pineapple chunks, onion rings (from marinade), cherry tomatoes, and bell pepper pieces.

5. Grill the skewers for 20–30 minutes, turning every 5 minutes.

# Stuffed Bell Peppers

## Ingredients

- 1 pound ground meat, preferably a mixture of any of the following: beef, lamb, pork, chicken, or turkey
- 4–6 bell peppers (you can use different colors)
- 1 small head of cauliflower, cut into uniform pieces
- 1 apple, peeled, cored, and finely shredded
- 1 onion, finely chopped
- 1 egg
- 1 tablespoon ghee (or fat of choice)
- 2–3 garlic cloves, minced
- 1 jar (7 ounces) of tomato paste
- Salt and pepper to taste

## Preparation

1. Cut stem and leaves off cauliflower. Using a food processor, shred the cauliflower into pieces the size of grains of rice.

2. In a bowl, mix meat, cauliflower, egg, apple, onion, garlic, salt, and pepper.

3. Cut off the tops of the bell peppers. Remove the seeds, and stuff the peppers with the mixture. Replace the pepper tops.

4. Carefully place peppers vertically into a pot.

5. Add ghee, tomato paste, and a pinch of salt to the pot with the stuffed peppers.

6. Add hot water to about ⅔ of the height of the peppers.

7. Cover with a lid and cook in preheated oven at 300°F for 1 hour.

# Faux Mashed Potatoes with Pears

## Ingredients

- 1 large head of cauliflower, cut into uniform pieces
- 2 pears
- 2–3 tablespoons ghee
- 1 cinnamon stick
- Grated rind of 1 lemon
- 1 clove
- Salt to taste

## Preparation

1. Quarter pears; remove cores and stems. Cut in long pieces.
2. In a small pot, melt ghee. Add pears, cinnamon stick, clove, and lemon rind.
3. Cover and sauté for 10–15 minutes.
4. Cut stem and leaves off cauliflower. Steam cauliflower; transfer to a bowl. Add salt. Mash with stick blender/potato masher.
5. Transfer cauliflower and pears to a deep serving dish, alternating the layers. Finish with a cauliflower layer, and top with hot ghee.

# Heidrek's Poached Salmon

## Ingredients

- 3 salmon steaks, cut 1-inch thick
- 3 cups water
- 1 tablespoon leeks, finely chopped
- 2 bay leaves
- 2 sprigs of parsley
- 2 sprigs of dill
- 2 lemons
- 2–3 cloves of garlic, minced
- 2 tablespoons ghee
- Salt and pepper to taste

## Preparation

1. Put water, leeks, bay leaves, parsley, dill, garlic, ghee, salt, and pepper into a deep skillet and bring to a simmer.
2. Add juice of 2 freshly squeezed lemons. Toss lemon peels in as well.
3. Add the salmon.
4. Cover the skillet and simmer over low heat for 8–10 minutes.
5. Serve salmon with faux mashed potatoes.

# Treats

# Chunky Fruit Ice Pops

## Ingredients

- 1 ripe mashed banana

- 1 cup chopped pineapple

- 1 cup chopped strawberries

- 1 can (13.5 ounces) full-fat coconut milk

- 1 teaspoon vanilla extract

## Preparation

1. In a bowl, mix mashed banana, coconut milk, and vanilla extract.

2. Add chunks of pineapple and strawberries to the mix.

3. Pour into molds and freeze.

# Apple Ice Cream

## Ingredients

- 3 ripe bananas, frozen
- 1 apple, peeled, cored, cut, and frozen
- 1 can (13.5 ounces) coconut cream, chilled
- 1 teaspoon vanilla extract
- 3 egg yolks
- ¼ cup fresh berries for topping

## Preparation

1. In a food processor or blender, mix all ingredients except berries.
2. Transfer the mixture into an ice-cream maker and prepare according to the machine's instructions.
3. Serve ice cream topped with fresh berries.

# Baked Apples

## Ingredients

- 4 large apples
- ½ cup dry fruit (raisins, chopped mango/apricots)
- ½ cup chopped walnuts
- ½ teaspoon ground cinnamon
- ¼ teaspoon ground nutmeg
- Dash of chili powder
- 1 lemon
- 2 tablespoons ghee

## Preparation

1. In a bowl, mix dry fruit, walnuts, cinnamon, nutmeg, and chili powder.
2. Peel the apples. Cut off the tops of the apples and carefully remove cores.
3. Rub the apples with lemon juice.
4. Fill apples with the prepared mixture.
5. Replace the apple tops.
6. Put some ghee on top of each apple.
7. Bake in preheated oven at 300°F for 30–45 minutes.
8. Serve with Apple Ice Cream.

# Kiwi Snowballs

## Ingredients

- 3 kiwis
- 3½ cups shredded coconut
- 2 tablespoons honey
- 8–10 hazelnuts

## Preparation

1. Peel kiwis.
2. In a food processor, mix the kiwis, honey, and 2½ cups of shredded coconut.
3. Using the mixture, make balls the size of a walnut.
4. Put 1 hazelnut inside of each ball—cut the ball in half, and place the hazelnut in the middle. Then put the two halves together and roll again.
5. Roll the balls in shredded coconut.
6. Refrigerate for a few hours and serve chilled.

# Lemon-Almond Cookies

## Ingredients

- 1 cup almonds
- Zest and juice of ½ a lemon
- 2 tablespoons honey
- 2 tablespoons melted ghee
- 1 tablespoon sesame seeds (optional)
- Pinch of salt

## Preparation

1. Process almonds in a powerful blender into almond flour. Transfer to a bowl.
2. Add remaining ingredients. Mix.
3. Form small, flat, round cookies and place them on a baking sheet.
4. Bake in preheated oven at 350°F for about 10 minutes, or until cookies become golden brown.
5. Take out of the oven and cool on a wire rack.

The cavekids return in:

# Fun Paleo Cooking Blog

cavekidscometodinner.com

Made in the USA
San Bernardino, CA
19 July 2016